The Escaped Pig

Watch out for these escaped pigs!

Lee Sterrey

Written by

Lee Sterrey

Illustrated by

Nicola Wyldbore-Smith

First published: November 2015

ISBN-10: 1499610025

ISBN-13: 978-1499610024

For my children, Dylan and Amber,

who always help to catch the pigs when they escape.

What's that digging sound?

It's coming from all around…

In a pen, behind a gate,

"Dig!" said Pig, "I want to escape!"

"I'm a big pig and need a big hole."

"But how do you dig without claws?" asked Mole.

Pig grunted. "Don't you know? I use my snout!

It's all I need to get out!"

With a squeeze and a push, Pig was free!

"Done! Now run!" squealed Pig with glee.

What's that *rumbling* sound?

Around the shed came a MASSIVE hound!

With droopy jaws and huge paws, now you know…

It's the thundering paws of Piccolo!

But, what's that *clipping* sound?

A MAGNIFICENT filly followed the hound.

With tossing mane and swishing tail, now you know…

It's the skipping hooves of Pogo!

In the farm, the Pig ran,

Piccolo and Pogo chase as best as they can.

"He is a fast hog, but I'm a fast filly,

I'm sure to catch him without looking silly."

Pig teased, "Some animals have handles. I have not!

It's what you need and I haven't got!"

With a snort and a squeal Pig ran free,

"Run! It's fun! You can't catch me!"

But what's that *wheezing* sound?

It wasn't coming from horse or hound.

With a sore trotter and aching leg, the pig stopped still,

No longer enjoying the fast-paced thrill.

But what's that *dragging* sound?

Of something being pulled along the ground.

With collar and lead, Piccolo tried to pull Pig.

"It's no good." sighed Piccolo, "He is just too big."

On a rooftop way up high,

Sat Snowy the cat with a watchful eye.

"You are a silly filly and a silly pup!

Dragging a pig won't bring you luck."

Snowy meowed, "Don't you know how to get Pig to move?

All you need is tasty food!

Now use apples and tempt the hog home,

Again to his pen, where he should roam."

What's that *munching* sound?

It's Pig eating apples off the ground!

With Piccolo and Pogo, who led to his pen,

Where he shall roam, once again.

But what's that *groaning* sound?

It's coming from all around.

With a tummy that feels funny, Pig slumps against the gate,

Eaten too many apples to try to escape!

More Adventures on Honey Bee Farm

Doyley the Dormouse

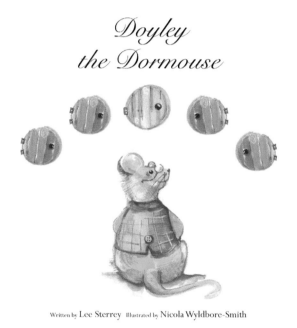

Written by Lee Sterrey Illustrated by Nicola Wyldbore-Smith

Doyley the Dormouse is the best door-maker in town, but how does he make one that isn't round?

www.facebook.com/DoyleytheDormouse

A note from the Author, Lee Sterrey:

The Escaped Pig was inspired by a true story that happened on our English hobby farm, where one of our Berkshire pigs escaped by digging under the gate. Pigs are very difficult to catch as they are very strong and can slip out of grasp very easily.
Piccolo really did try to help with a lead - but in the end it was the bucket of apples that we used to get the pig back home!

About the Berkshire pig:
Berkshire pigs are a UK rare-breed that are covered in thick black hair, typically with a white stripe on their face and white trotters (feet). Unlike commercial pig breeds, they are smaller, which makes them a little bit easier to handle. They tend to be very friendly and my children love playing games with them.

To see photos and videos of animals on the farm, visit the website:
www.AdventuresOnHoneyBeeFarm.com

About the illustrator, Nicola Wyldbore-Smith

Nicola gains much of her inspiration for her illustrations from the beautiful Warwickshire (UK) countryside in which she resides. Having kept many animals including horses, sheep and dogs she captures the natural movement and expressions of animals in her illustrations.

For Adventures on Honey Bee Farm stories, Nicola creates her drawings first in pencil and then uses watercolour paints to get that lovely delicate finish that can only be obtained by hand painting.

Each finished artwork is a masterpiece in it's own right.

Made in the USA
Charleston, SC
10 December 2015